To Bluejay
—GH

For Dan, with love
—CM & BM

EAGLE BOY

A Traditional Navajo Legend Retold by

Gerald Hausman

Illustrated by Cara and Barry Moser

HarperCollins*Publishers*

Acknowledgments

The author wishes to thank Jay DeGroat, Bluejay, for helping him to understand the Navajo Ways. In addition, he would like to thank the Wheelwright Museum of the American Indian for permission to use the personal papers of Mary C. Wheelwright. The original source for Eagle Boy came from a long ceremonial recitation of the Navajo Beadway, told by Yohe Hatrali and recorded by Ms. Wheelwright. The author adapted a small part of the eagle legend and retold it in the shape of this book.

The text display type for Eagle Boy *was composed in Tiepolo. The paintings were executed in pastel on board. The transparencies were made by Gamma One Conversions, New York, New York. The color separations were made by Imago/Bright Arts. The entire book was printed on 80# Patina made by S.D. Warren Company. Production supervision by Lucille Schneider and Lisa Ford. Designed by Barry Moser, Cara Moser, and Christine Kettner.*

Library of Congress Cataloging-in-Publication Data   Hausman, Gerald.   Eagle boy : a traditional Navajo legend / retold by Gerald Hausman ; illustrated by Cara and Barry Moser.   p.   cm.   Summary: Father and Mother Eagle take a Navajo boy to the country of the clouds where, though he allows Coyote to trick him, he learns the healing ways of eagles.   ISBN 0-06-021100-8. — ISBN 0-06-021101-6 (lib. bdg.)
1. Navajo Indians—Legends.   [1. Navajo Indians—Legends.   2. Indians of North America—Legends.]
I. Moser, Barry, ill.   II. Moser, Cara, ill.   III. Title. E99.N3H37   1996   91-47988   398.21'089972—dc20
CIP [E] AC

EAGLE BOY

Once

there was a boy who dreamed of eagles. He pictured them flying in the sky over his hogan, their shadows slipping easily across the soft red sand. One morning, Father Eagle came and caught him by the shirt and carried him to a nest far up on the side of a cliff. The boy peered over the cliff edge at his mother and father standing in front of the hogan. They were so small he could barely see them. He knew that this was not a dream, but something that was really happening to him.

"You are like one of us," Father Eagle said. "For this reason we are going to take you to the eagle people who live at the top of the sky."

"But I am hungry," the boy said. "I did not have breakfast."

"Very well," replied Father Eagle. And he brought a yellow bowl from under his right wing. "Try this," he offered. "It is sacred cornmeal mixed with water."

The boy thanked Father Eagle and dipped in his finger. "This is what we eat at home," he said.

After a while, Mother Eagle came down out of the clouds. "Here," she said. "I have brought you some food,"

and she gave the boy her bowl of sacred cornmeal. This cornmeal was many colored, sparkling like a rainbow. He started to take it, but Mother Eagle stopped him. "We eat with our wing," she told him. "You should use your hand."

The boy stopped dipping his finger into the cornmeal and began to scoop it up with his whole hand.

When he had finished, Mother Eagle showed him the four blankets of the eagle people. The first was made of darkness. The second was morning dawn. The third was red afterglow. The fourth was blue afterglow. "We shall wrap you up in these," Mother Eagle explained, "and then we will carry you into the clouds."

Father Eagle gave the boy a rock crystal that glowed when he touched it. "Hold on to the rock crystal," he instructed, "and you will be able to see through the sacred blankets."

Mother Eagle gave the boy a sheep's horn that had two holes at either end. "Put the horn over your mouth," she told him, "and after we wrap you up, you will be able to breathe."

After this, the eagles robed him in darkness, morning dawn, red afterglow, and blue afterglow. When he was bundled up, they carried him away into the sky.

The boy held on to the rock crystal, and though it was dark down deep in the blankets, he could see the clear sky through them. And with the sheep's horn pressed to his lips, he could breathe the fresh air. They went higher and higher, the wind grew louder, and the eagles had to flap their wings very hard.

Soon they reached the top of the sky. Father Eagle made the eagle call, and Chicken Hawk appeared and cut a hole in the clouds. All the eagle people were waiting on the other side, and they helped to carry the boy until, at last,

they put him down and unwrapped him. First they took off the blanket of blue afterglow, then red afterglow, then morning dawn, and darkness. The boy stepped out into the country of clouds at the top of the sky.

He was greeted by Chicken Hawk, Eagle Chief, Big Black Eagle, Yellow-Tailed Eagle, Buzzard, and others. They liked the boy, and they welcomed him to their home. Mother Eagle told him, "You will stay here with Eagle Chief in his white cloud house to the east."

"And remember," Father Eagle said, "to do what Eagle Chief tells you to do. He is very wise and knows what is best."

The boy promised to do this, and he thanked Father Eagle and Mother Eagle for bringing him to the cloud country. After saying good-bye, they flew home through the hole in the clouds.

Eagle Chief took the boy to his great white cloud house in the east. "You will be happy here," he said, "but you must stay inside when I am gone." Then Eagle Chief left, and the boy was alone.

At first he found things to amuse himself. Eagle Chief had prayer sticks and rattles and big drums. But when he finished looking at all of these, he wanted to go outside. It was bright and sunny, and the clouds were stacked up like mesas. He looked out the window of Eagle Chief's cloud house and saw a funny-looking animal sitting on a rock of clouds.

"I will just open the door and take a peek at him," the boy thought to himself. But when he opened the door, Big Wind blew it all the way open. The boy was pulled outside.

The funny-looking animal called out, "Boy, are you afraid of me?" The boy looked over and knew who it was: Coyote, the trickster!

"Are you afraid of your cousin?" Coyote asked the boy.

"I'm not afraid of you," the boy replied bravely.

"If you are not afraid, come over so we can have a little talk," said Coyote.

When the boy reached him, Coyote said, "Touch my fur."

"Why?" the boy asked.

"Because up here in the clouds, my fur turns into rain sprinkles that are so soft you can hardly feel them."

The boy put out his hand, and as he touched the white-gold fur, the trickster disappeared. The boy himself turned into a skinny coyote.

"Come back!" the boy called, or thought he did. He could not tell, for his voice had changed. But he received no answer.

Soon Eagle Chief returned, but he could not find the boy anywhere. "Where has that earth boy gone to?" he asked Dragonfly.

Dragonfly chuckled, "You have been looking right at him."

"All I see is a skinny coyote," Eagle Chief protested. Then he called Little Wind. "Where has that earth boy gone to?" he asked.

Little Wind laughed. "You are looking at him."

"All I see," Eagle Chief repeated, "is a skinny coyote." Then he realized what had happened. The boy had disobeyed him, and Coyote had tricked him.

"All right," Eagle Chief said, "I know what must be done." And he carved four soft hoops out of tree branches and gave them to four of the eagle people to hold in their beaks. Eagle Chief lined them up, one after the other, and called out to the boy, "Jump through the first hoop." The boy did, and his head turned back into his own.

"Now jump through the second hoop," Eagle Chief directed. The boy did, and his arms turned back into his own. "Now jump through the third hoop," Eagle Chief told him. The boy did, and his legs, except his ankles and feet, turned into his own.

"Now jump through the fourth hoop," Eagle Chief said. The boy did, and after passing through the fourth hoop, he was himself again.

"How did it happen that you left my cloud house?" Eagle Chief asked the boy.

"I was tricked by Coyote," the boy said.

"And by yourself," Eagle Chief added. "Now you must return to your home, and tell the earth people how you jumped through our hoops and got rid of Coyote's magic. But before you go, you must promise never to be tricked again."

"I promise," the boy answered.

So Eagle Chief gave the boy a sacred eagle feather and a new name to carry with him back to earth. "Your new name shall be Eagle Boy," Eagle Chief announced, and the boy was pleased because a name given by a chief has great power.

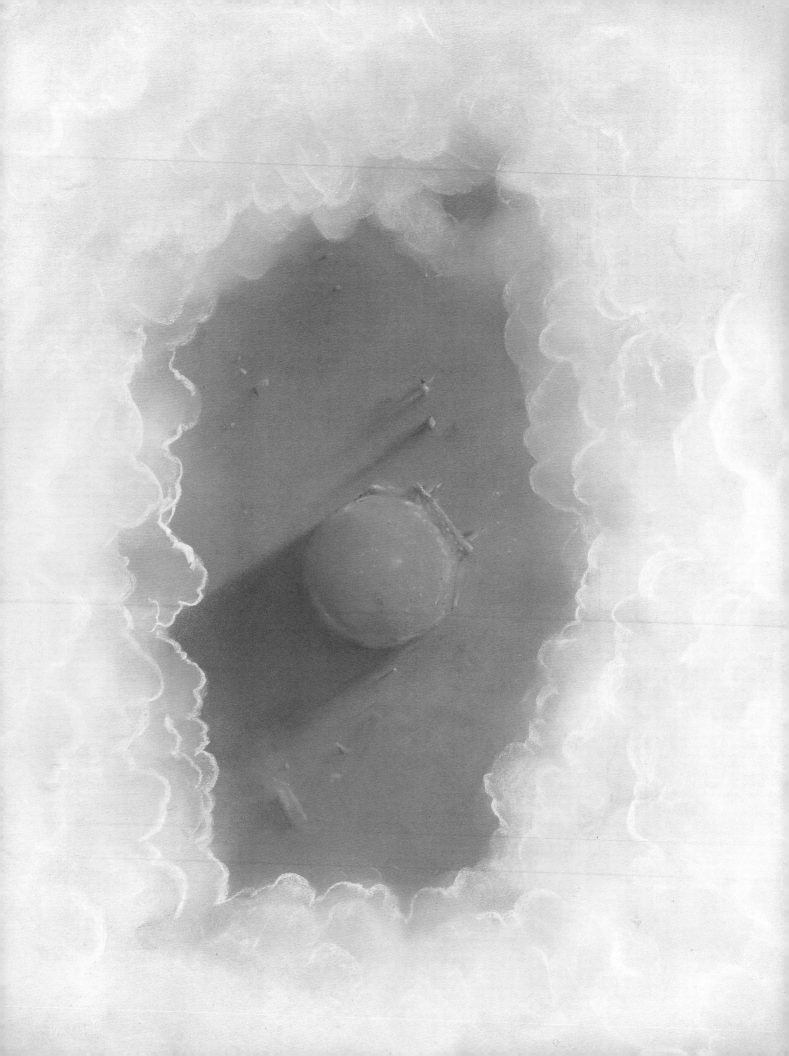

Eagle Chief picked up Rolling Tumbleweed and cast him through the clouds, and a hole was made so that Eagle Boy could see all the way down to earth. Far below, on the red sand of the desert, he saw his family's hogan. His mother and father were standing outside, waiting for him to come home.

"How will I return to them?" Eagle Boy asked.

"Hold tight to the sacred feather," Eagle Chief replied. Then he blew on it four times, and Eagle Boy felt something buzzing under his feet. He was lifted off the clouds and carried through the hole made by Rolling Tumbleweed.

Eagle Boy saw his friend, Eagle Chief, wave good-bye to him. The buzzing under his feet grew louder and warmer, and he fell through the sky, holding tightly to the sacred feather.

On the way down he saw many of his new friends: eagles, chicken hawks, and buzzards. He did not let go of the feather, and soon he landed in front of his hogan. He fell so softly that his parents, who were looking the other way, did not even hear him.

"Here I am," cried Eagle Boy. "I have come all the way from my visit with the eagle people."

His mother and father were happy to see their son. "With that sacred feather," his father said, "you will become a great medicine man."

"Yes," his mother agreed, pointing down at Eagle Boy's feet, "but what will you do with those two bumblebees?"

"Bumblebees?" Eagle Boy asked. He looked down at his

moccasins and saw a bumblebee under each foot. "So that is why my feet are buzzing!"

"And that is why my little boy fell to earth without hurting himself," said his mother.

"That is not the only reason," Eagle Boy said. "It is because I have a new name, given to me by Eagle Chief!" Then he told them his name, and they praised him for having it.

And they turned and went into the hogan, and the two bumblebees buzzed back up into the clouds.

Eagle Boy did not forget what he had learned, and when he grew up, he became a great medicine man.

Author's Note

The story of Eagle Boy comes from the Navajo Eagle Way. There are many Navajo Ways, all of them healing ceremonies, used by medicine men to make people well. Long ago, when a Navajo person had a sore throat, a headache, or even a swollen leg, a medicine man was often called upon to perform an Eagle Way.

To the Navajo, eagles represent more than the power of flight. They are considered sacred, godlike birds. When a medicine man does an Eagle Way, he sings eagle songs and makes a sand painting depicting the world of the eagles. The purpose of the painting, made of colored sand from the desert, is to bring the patient nearer to the healing power of the eagle people. By sitting on the sand painting, the one who is ill "visits" with the eagles, receiving their blessing so that he, or she, can get well again.

The story of Eagle Boy tells how, in the beginning, the first Navajo learned the ways of the eagles by going on a journey into the sky. When he returned, he taught his people how to do the eagle dance and sing the eagle songs. In so doing, he became a great medicine man.

—G H